The Puppy who was Left Behind

Holly Webb

Illustrated by Sophy Williams

Stripes

See page 128 for a glossary of boat words.

For Maddison

For more information about Holly Webb visit:
www.holly-webb.com

STRIPES PUBLISHING
An imprint of Little Tiger Press
1 The Coda Centre, 189 Munster Road,
London SW6 6AW

A paperback original
First published in Great Britain in 2013

ISBN: 978-1-84715-373-9

A CIP catalogue record for this book is available from the British Library.

Printed and bound in the UK.

10 9 8 7 6 5 4 3 2 1

Chapter One

"I'm ready to go!" Anna raced into the kitchen, dragging her wheelie suitcase, with a rucksack on her back. Her Irish Setter puppy, Fred, galloped behind her. He was very confused by the suitcase, but he liked the way it rattled.

"Are you really all packed?" Mum asked, looking at Anna's bags. "That was quick. What are you taking?"

Anna peered behind her at the suitcase and laughed at Fred. He was trying to get his nose underneath to nibble at the wheels.

"Um, I can't think of anything else to pack. Gran said not to bring loads. There isn't a lot of space on the canal boat, so I've just got my jeans, some shorts and a couple of T-shirts and a sweater. But you're coming over to visit on Sunday, anyway, aren't you? So you can bring me some more clothes if I need them."

Then she gasped. "Oh, but I need to pack for Fred! I didn't think about that." She looked doubtfully at her suitcase. There was no way Fred's food and bowls were going to fit in there, let alone all his toys. And his cushion.

Her mum laughed. "I think your gran might not mind if he brought his own bag. Just not too many toys, OK?"

Anna sighed. It was going to be hard to choose which ones to take. She was always buying Fred things with her pocket money, so he had loads of toys. His favourites were definitely all the ones that squeaked – he would play with them for ages. If Anna was too busy to throw them for him to fetch, he would do it himself. He'd worked out that he could swing his toy around in his teeth and let go, then he would chase it down the hallway and fling himself at it, skidding along on the smooth wooden floor.

Perhaps she could set out a line-up for him and see which ones he chose? But then his favourite seemed to change every day.

"Come and have some breakfast," her mum suggested. "We need to set off for the boat pretty soon."

Anna put the bags in the hallway, and then returned to the kitchen, giving her mum a hug as she came in.

"Oh! That was nice, what was that for?" her mum asked, hugging her back tightly.

"I'll miss you, that's all. And Dad. I'm really looking forward to staying on the boat with Gran and Grandad, but it'll be the first time I've stayed away without you."

"You'll have a lovely time," her mum said reassuringly. "And you're only on the boat tomorrow and Saturday before we come and see you."

"I'll have Fred as well!" Anna smiled, pouring cornflakes into her bowl and reaching for the milk jug.

Fred, who had been sniffing at one of his rubber bones that had somehow managed to get itself wedged under the fridge, leaped up excitedly as he heard his name. Anna was calling him!

He darted over to the table, skidding

like he always did on the smooth floor, and hurled himself lovingly at Anna's legs.

Anna squeaked and tipped the milk. It flooded over the edge of her bowl and across the table, dripping all over Fred's feathery, dark red fur.

He looked up at her, his big dark eyes confused. Why was he all wet? What had happened? He shook himself, and drops of milk went all over the kitchen.

"Oh, Fred..." Mum and Anna groaned at the same time. It was something they said quite a lot.

"I hope he's going to be all right on the boat," Mum went on. "It's such a small space, and he isn't very good at being cooped up, is he?"

Anna looked down at her puppy, who was now licking the milky drops off his nose with a thoughtful expression. Then he gazed up at the table again, obviously wondering how to get himself some more.

"No!" Anna moved the bowl away from the edge of the table and shook her head at him sternly. Mum was right. Fred was a wide open spaces sort of dog. They'd known before they got him that Irish Setters needed lots of exercise – at least one really good long walk (or run, really) every day. Plus it was best if they had a garden to run around in.

That was partly why they'd chosen to get an Irish Setter, when they'd all talked about what sort of dog they'd like. Anna had originally thought it would be fun to have a tiny dog, like a Chihuahua. She'd imagined sneaking the puppy into her backpack and taking him to school. But her dad had pointed out that a Chihuahua probably wouldn't be able to walk very far, and what they wanted was a dog to go on brilliant walks with.

Although their house was in a town, it was right on the edge and there was a big, wild sort of park close to where they lived. Then, if they got in the car, it only took about ten minutes to drive to a huge wood that they could explore.

And the only thing that would make all their walks even better was a dog…

Anna hadn't minded not having a Chihuahua as soon as Dad had showed her the email from the lady who had the Irish Setter puppies for sale. There were photos attached and they were so gorgeous. Anna didn't think she'd ever seen an Irish Setter before and she had never imagined a dog that colour – a sort of dark, autumn-leaves red, but with such a shine to it.

In the best photo, the puppies were all asleep, squashed up together in a basket so that Anna could hardly tell where one puppy ended and another began. Random paws and ears were sticking out all over the place, and one of the puppies was nearly falling out of the basket, but was so deeply asleep that he hadn't even noticed.

When they went to see the puppies a couple of days later, Anna was sure that she could tell which one had been half out of the basket. He had the same huge, curly-haired ears. And when he had curled up in Anna's lap and stretched himself luxuriously, his paws stuck out in that same clumsy way. As Anna ran her hand over his soft head, and he yawned and snuggled deeper into her fleece, she had known that he was just the right puppy for them.

Anna looked down at Fred – he was so much bigger now. "I'll be able to take him for long walks along the towpath, won't I?" she said to Mum. "He'll love that. He might even want to swim! Irish Setters are supposed to be good in the water." She reached down and stroked his ears. "I bet you'd be a great swimmer, wouldn't you?"

Mum looked at the puppy, sipping her tea. "Actually, I'm not sure that's such a good idea. The canal banks are pretty steep at the sides – they go straight down into the water. If Fred jumps in, he might have a hard time getting out again. And the canal's deep. Fred's probably better off waiting until we go to the seaside for his first swim." She grinned at Anna. "Then he can go into the sea with you!"

"Mmmm." Anna nodded. "I hadn't thought about how he'd get out again. I hope he doesn't want to jump off the boat. But Sunny never does that, does he?"

Sunny was Gran and Grandad's black Labrador. He always went with them on their canal boat, the *Hummingbird*. He would sit in the bow or on the roof posing, with a noble expression on his face, so people on the towpath always wanted to take photos of him. He was also very, very well-trained. Anna and Mum had taken Fred to training classes, and he was pretty good, but he was a still a bit of a scatty pup compared to perfect Sunny. Anna was fairly certain that if she put a delicious plate of sausages down in front of Sunny and told him to guard it, he would stay there watching the sausages for ever, if necessary. He wouldn't even sniff at them.

Fred, on the other hand, would wolf the sausages down in seconds, but Anna didn't really mind. She did worry that when she let Fred off the lead she wasn't always sure if he'd come back again. At least, not if there was something more interesting going on – like a really nice bit of rubbish he wanted to eat first.

Dad said it was all about the voice, and Anna just had to try and sound firmer. But Anna had noticed that Fred didn't always come back first time for Dad, either.

Chapter Two

"So are you ready to get going?" Grandad asked, smiling at Anna.

Anna nodded excitedly. She was standing on the bank, ready to cast off the mooring ropes. And Grandad was at the tiller, about to start the engine. They were going to set sail at last!

Mum had had to head home after lunch and a quick cup of tea. She was an illustrator and she had a lot of work on at the moment, which was why Anna was coming to stay on the boat. She could have stayed at home, but Mum wouldn't have been able to do anything very exciting with her, and Dad was out at work every day. Anna didn't really fancy spending the time just watching TV or lounging around in the garden.

She would have loved to go off exploring with Fred, but Mum and Dad weren't happy about her being on her own. Anna had tried to argue that Fred would be with her, but it hadn't convinced them. Fred hadn't helped much, either. He'd walked in while they were talking, carrying his lead as though he were an angelic dog. But when Anna had taken it out of his mouth, the lead had fallen apart, because he'd chewed it all the way through. After that it was quite hard to claim that Fred was super-sensible and they would be fine…

Luckily, Gran and Grandad were spending the summer on their canal boat, the *Hummingbird*, and were going to be passing quite close to where Anna and her parents lived. They'd happened to ring up for one of their regular chats, and Gran had asked Anna if she was looking forward to the summer holidays.

"Sort of," Anna had told her doubtfully. "But Mum's got to work for the first bit of the holidays so she can get everything done before we go away."

"Oh yes, she did tell me that," said

Gran. "She's got a big piece of work to finish off, hasn't she?"

"Yes." Anna sighed. "It'll be nice not having to get up and go to school, but it isn't really going to feel like the holidays. Not if we can't go out and do stuff. Usually we do trips and go off on our bikes with a picnic. Mum says she'll try and arrange for me to go and see Lucy and Jenna – you know, my friends from school. But it isn't the same if we can't have them back round to our house, too."

"Mmm, I see what you mean..." Gran said thoughtfully. "Anna, I'll have to ask your mum and dad, of course, but would you like to come and stay on the boat with us for a few days? That would give your mum lots of time to get her work done and you wouldn't be stuck inside all day."

"Just me?" Anna gasped. "On the boat? Oh, I'd love it! Would we actually get to sail? I mean, we wouldn't just be moored up on the bank?"

"Of course! Your mum and dad could drop you off, and then pick you up again a few days later, somewhere further down the canal."

"Fantastic!" Anna said gleefully. "Oh… Oh, but Gran, I've just thought. What about Fred? I was planning to play with him lots in the garden. Mum's going to be so busy – she said he'd just have to make do with a couple of short walks every day. If he's just with Mum and there's no one to play with him, he'll get all naughty and jumpy and start chewing things. Well," she added honestly, remembering the lead, "I mean, he'll chew things even more than he does already."

"Yes, I'd forgotten about Fred." Gran was silent for a moment, and Anna could tell she was thinking. "I don't see why you couldn't bring him, too. You could take him for some lovely runs along the towpath. Perhaps you could race me and Grandad in the boat!"

Anna giggled. She would probably win. Canal boats were good, but they weren't really built for getting anywhere fast.

She had passed the phone over to her mum, with a pleading, hopeful look, and it had all been arranged. Mum would drop off Anna and Fred at the boat on Thursday, the first day of the holidays, and she would stay for a week.

Anna had been to visit her grandparents on the boat before, but only for the day, and they had always stayed on the mooring – more like being in a house than a boat. So she was really excited to be setting off down the canal at last.

She heard the rumble of the engine starting up. Grandad was getting ready for them to pull away from the bank! Fred nuzzled the back of her knee with his cold nose and whined. Anna had kept him on his lead – there wasn't a lot of space on the boat, and even though Fred was only five months old, he was already getting big. His long, plumy tail was just at the right height to sweep Gran's ornaments off the shelves set into the side of the saloon – the boat's little living room. Plus everyone seemed to keep falling over him, especially Grandad. He'd tripped over Fred at least twice, and then when Fred hid under the table, Grandad trod on his tail, which was sticking out.

But Anna's real worry was the water. Even though it was a beautiful day, the canal still looked freezing. And deep. Anna wasn't tempted to swim in it at all, but she had a horrible feeling that Fred might be.

When they'd first climbed into the little well deck at the front of the boat, he kept trying to lean over the side, sniffing excitedly at the water. Anna didn't quite understand what it was that smelled so good, but then she didn't think it was fun to eat slugs, either, which were another of Fred's favourites.

It didn't help that ducks kept swimming past and circling hopefully round the bow of the boat, just in case anyone fancied throwing them some bread.

The first time he saw the ducks, Fred

froze, so excited he could hardly move. Once he'd decided they were actually real and not something that he'd dreamed up, he let out three huge, ear-splitting barks and yanked as hard as he could on his lead. He scrabbled frantically at the side of the boat with his claws, trying to throw himself overboard to catch the tempting feathery things.

"Fred!" Anna gasped, clutching at his lead. "Hey, come back!"

The ducks suddenly found something interesting to go and look at close to the other bank, and Mum had grabbed hold of Fred's collar, helping Anna to haul him back.

Fred carried on growling for a bit, before he finally gave up and accepted that they'd gone.

"Wow..." Anna muttered. "I didn't think about ducks. He was almost straight in. Is there such a thing as a dog lifejacket?"

She had a lifejacket on herself – Gran had explained that they knew she wasn't silly enough to fall in, but accidents did sometimes happen and it was better to be safe.

"I'm sure you can get them. Does Sunny have a lifejacket?" Mum asked, glancing over at the black Labrador, who was sunbathing on the roof of the boat. He was asleep, or he seemed to be, but Anna noticed he had one eye half-open, as though he was keeping watch. She had a feeling he was partly watching for Fred, in case he did something awful.

Gran shook her head. "No... He's actually a very good swimmer. And he's so sensible, we've never thought we needed one."

Anna sighed. "Was Sunny sensible even when he was a puppy?"

"I think he was..." Grandad frowned, trying to remember.

Anna nodded. It made sense. She found it difficult to imagine perfectly behaved Sunny as a puppy at all!

Gran shook her head. "He certainly wasn't! Don't you remember my best pink shoes?"

Grandad laughed. "Yes! How could I forget?"

Gran sighed. "Oh, they were lovely, those shoes. I still miss them. He chewed one of them to pieces! The other shoe was still perfect and somehow that made it even worse!" She gave Anna a hug and rubbed Fred's ears. "Fred will settle down, don't worry. I don't think Irish Setters are quite as … obedient as Labradors, but he just needs to grow up a bit."

Anna nodded gratefully, feeling a bit better. She looked up at Sunny, trying to imagine him with a pink shoe dangling out of his mouth.

Sunny snorted a little and laid his nose on his paws, as though he'd never done anything like that in his life.

Fred gave up on the ducks after that. He didn't understand why he wasn't allowed off the lead. Usually when they went out to the woods or the park, he could go racing away. He loved to run, but there wasn't a lot of running space on the boat. It was only a few paces wide, for a start. And there wasn't a hallway to race up and down like there was at home. There didn't seem to be a garden either, only the long pathway at the edge of the water.

Fred was just as unsure about the water as Anna was. He'd never seen so much of it in one place before and he definitely thought it looked cold, too. But when he'd seen the ducks, somehow he forgot to worry about that.

He peered up at Sunny, who was still snoozing on the roof. He didn't understand how Sunny could sleep through the loud rattling rumble of the engine. Perhaps he was just used to it. If Sunny would only wake up, maybe they could go running together. Fred was pretty sure he would be the fastest. He always was.

Sunny was watching him, Fred

realized. This was his boat, Fred could smell that it was. He huffed and turned round on Anna's feet so that he wasn't looking at the bigger dog any more.

He was starting to wish they were back home.

Chapter Three

By the end of the day, Fred seemed to settle down to being on the boat. Anna had brought along his big cushion to make him feel more at home. Fred leaped on to it gratefully when Anna put it out next to her bed.

Anna had been a bit confused as to where she would actually sleep when Gran had invited her to stay on the boat, because she could only remember there being one double bedroom. She'd thought she might have to sleep in her sleeping bag on the floor somewhere, but Gran had laughed and promised her a proper bed.

That evening she explained that boats were all about saving space, and showed Anna how the table in the kitchen area folded down and the benches on either side of it slid round to make a comfy little bed. It was very clever. And it meant that Anna and Fred drifted off to sleep that night with Gran and Grandad sitting in their armchairs, watching television, but with the sound turned down so low that it mixed with the soft lapping of the water against the hull.

Anna dreamed of floating off across the water in a tiny bed.

On Friday everyone woke up early. Anna did as Gran suggested and took Fred for two lovely long runs, racing the boat. They could run just as fast as the *Hummingbird*, as the part of the canal they were on had a five-mile-an-hour speed limit, which was a good sort of speed to keep up.

Anna could tell that Fred was feeling better after all that exercise. By the time they stopped at one of the locks late that afternoon, and Anna helped Grandad open the lock gates, he was slumped in the long grass, panting happily. Anna had to coax him up and on to the boat. Then he made straight for his big cushion, flopping down on to it.

Anna laughed. Fred still slept the way he had when he was a puppy, all legs sticking out everywhere. It did mean he took up a lot of room inside the boat. They kept having to step round him. But he was very sweet and he wasn't being naughty, so no one minded.

Anna did wish that Fred got on better with Sunny, though. Actually, it didn't really seem to be Fred's fault. He was always very friendly with other dogs, even smaller ones, and he loved to chase and play and romp up and down the park with them. He even had a couple of "best friends" – a spaniel called Lottie and a tiny Jack Russell called Max, who bossed Fred and Lottie around all the time.

Anna had thought that Fred and Sunny would probably get on in the same sort of way. She'd even imagined that it would be a nice treat for Sunny to have another dog for company.

Unfortunately, Sunny didn't seem to see it that way. He'd never shared his house or his boat with another dog, and he didn't see why he had to start now. Especially with a dog like this, who frisked around everywhere the whole time, and kept sniffing at him and creeping up on him and yapping excitedly. Sunny didn't like it at all and he snapped when Fred nuzzled at him, and let out a furious growl when the pup jumped into his basket. Fred jumped out again quickly, creeping away with his head hanging low and his back rounded in a shamed sort of crouch.

Fred was confused. He wasn't used to sharing his home either, but the other dogs in the park liked him to play. He was only doing what he always did.

Still, at least he had Anna. He'd dragged his cushion right up to her strange little bed on the first night, so that he could curl up close to her. In fact, that was one thing that was better than home – there he slept in the kitchen. Now he was close enough to hear her breathing, and for her to reach down a hand and stroke him sleepily.

The two long walks meant that Fred fell asleep early that night, curled up on Anna's feet as they ate dinner. He only really woke up long enough for a last quick trip out on to the towpath before Anna went to bed.

Fred woke up early Saturday morning, feeling full of energy. At home he would have scratched hopefully at the back door until someone let him out into the garden, or raced madly up and down the hallway, chasing his toys. But there just wasn't enough room for that here.

He gnawed fiercely at one of his rubber bones for a while – it was easy to find, as he discovered he'd been asleep on top of it. It wasn't as good as a walk, though. He sat up and stared hopefully at Anna, who was still sleeping. He put his paws up on the edge of the bed and whined, but she only made a strange sleepy noise and rolled over away from him.

Fred slumped back on to his cushion, and looked at Sunny, who was curled up in his basket on the other side of the saloon. Maybe Sunny would play? There wasn't a lot of room, but perhaps they could chase each other up and down?

He uncurled himself and crept over to Sunny's basket, whining a little.

Sunny woke up and stared grumpily at him, but Fred just thumped his huge feathery tail on the boards and put his head on one side, his ears twitching with excitement. Then he dropped down in front of the basket, stretching his paws out, and let out a few sharp yaps.

Sunny sat up and glared at him, and let out a furious growl.

Fred wriggled backwards, upset and a bit frightened. Why wouldn't Sunny play with him? He barked, suddenly and loudly, so that Anna woke up with a start and banged her head on a shelf. She yelped, rubbing the back of her head.

Fred panicked completely. Sunny was growling at him, and now Anna sounded upset, and he didn't understand what was going on. He ran backwards and forwards across the boat, barking and bumping into the shelves along the walls, and then the little folding table where Gran always put her tea.

The table went flying and banged against Fred's front leg. He whimpered and came to a stop. He crouched in the middle of the cabin, his paw held up miserably.

"What's going on?" Grandad came out of the bedroom, looking rumpled and sleepy and cross. "Is somebody hurt? What have you done, you silly dog!"

Fred whimpered again and wriggled backwards behind one of the armchairs. Grandad's voice was low and rumbly, and not like any of the voices that Fred was used to. He could tell that the deep-voiced person was very cross, and Anna was crying, and Sunny was still letting out low, furious growls. Now everyone was angry with him...

Chapter Four

"What on earth happened?" Gran asked, hurrying out of the bedroom and putting an arm around Anna. "Did you bump yourself, Anna? And where's Fred?"

"Over there," Anna sniffed, still rubbing her head. "Behind the armchair. I think he's hurt his paw – the table fell on it."

"Oh dear," Gran murmured. "Well, thank goodness there wasn't anything on it. It's lucky I moved that little vase yesterday. If that had smashed, he could have cut himself."

Grandad went over to pick up the table. "Not broken. It's fine. Come on out, Fred." He crouched down and looked round the armchair, but Fred had crept right behind it now. All that they could see was a dark pinkish nose and they could hear him whimpering. "Poor old boy. He's really scared." He sighed. "Sorry, Anna, that's probably my fault. I shouted and he doesn't really know me."

Anna slid down from the bed and hurried over to Fred's hiding place. "Hey, Fred. It's OK. Come on out."

Fred sniffed cautiously at Anna's outstretched hand and slowly, gradually, he wriggled out from behind the chair. But he was shivering and he still looked miserable. Anna carefully checked his paw, but it wasn't bleeding and it didn't seem to be hurting him any more.

"Oh dear." Gran sighed. "Was it another squabble with him and Sunny, do you think?"

"That's what it sounded like," Grandad agreed. "Lots of barking and scuffling. I suppose Sunny thinks it's his boat. He's never had another dog on board before. And he isn't used to a friendly puppy like Fred, all bounce and tail-wagging."

"What are we going to do?" Anna whispered. Grandad had picked up the table, but there were still newspapers everywhere and Fred had knocked over a pile of books. A couple of Gran's pretty china animals were on the floor, too, and Anna really hoped they hadn't been broken. The room was a mess.

Gran frowned. "I'm not sure. They really aren't getting on, are they? I know Fred's only trying to be friendly, but he's just got so much energy. He isn't the right sort of dog to be squashed up on a boat." She shook her head, worriedly. "I'm sorry, Anna, I didn't think about this properly. I was just so excited about you coming to stay with us."

Anna nodded and sniffed. "Do we have to go home?" she whispered. She didn't want to, but it wasn't fair on Gran and Grandad to have Fred spoiling their beautiful boat.

"I don't think it's that bad…" Gran murmured. "Let's all get dressed and have some breakfast. If you throw some clothes on quickly, you could take Fred for a quick walk, maybe? That'll cheer him up and burn off some of his energy. And your grandad and I can think about what to do."

Fred wagged his tail a little as he saw Anna pick up his lead. A walk. It was all he had wanted, really, but everything seemed to have gone wrong.

Still, as he hopped carefully over on to the bank and sniffed the cool morning air, everything seemed better. The grass was lovely and wet under his paws, and interesting things had been running along the towpath in the night – rabbits and those hard-to-catch ducks. He sniffed busily, nuzzling into the clumps of grass and under the brambly hedges.

"Come on, Fred," Anna said at last, yawning. "We should go back now. Don't you want your breakfast? I'm starving."

All the same, she walked slowly as they turned back towards the boat, letting Fred rootle around in the long grass. There were scuffling noises in the hedges and indignant twitterings. She smiled. "Watch it, Fred. You'll get your nose pecked in a minute, mister."

Even though Fred didn't like being shut up and he kept getting in trouble with Sunny, Anna loved being out here with him. She didn't want to go home.

But she couldn't see what else they could do.

"So, your mum and dad are coming over for lunch tomorrow," Grandad said, buttering his toast.

"Mmm..." Anna nodded. And they were going to say that she and Fred should go back home with them, she just knew it. She sighed.

"We were thinking perhaps they could take Fred home, too," Gran said.

Anna stared at her. "Just Fred? And leave me here?"

Gran and Grandad both nodded, and Anna glanced from one to the other, confused.

"But what about Mum? She won't be able to look after him properly. That's why I had to bring him. I mean, I wanted to, anyway, but it was mostly because he needs someone around."

Anna sniffed and shook her head apologetically. "I know he made a real mess of the boat, but if he didn't get walked enough at home, he'd probably do the same. He chews things when he's bored. If I'm home at least I can play with him in the garden."

"Ah, but you see, your mum's got loads of work done already," Gran explained. "She called me while you were on your walk with Fred. She said she was glad to hear you were having a lovely time on the boat and she didn't have to worry about you. I'm sure she'd be able to fit in walking Fred now she's got a bit more time."

"Oh..." Anna frowned to herself. If they both went back, her mum would be worrying about whether

Anna was all right, stuck at home while she was trying to work. "I suppose you're right," she murmured. She really didn't want Fred to go, but it did seem like the best solution. If you didn't count how much she would miss him.

Anna took Fred for another really long walk along the towpath that morning. Partly because she knew she was going to miss him so much after he went home tomorrow, but also because she was hoping, just a little bit, that if she wore him out enough, he'd be really good. Then maybe Gran and Grandad would change their minds and say it was OK for him to stay.

They moored up that afternoon next to a break in the woods that ran along one bank of the canal. The dark trees opened out and there was a huge field, dotted with big, old oak trees. Anna looked out at it delightedly. She couldn't wait to explore, and Fred's tail was wafting back and forth excitedly as he looked at all that open space to run in.

"It's beautiful!" Anna said to Grandad, as she helped him tie the boat up to the mooring posts on the bank. Fred was pulling hopefully at his lead, as though he wanted to go for a walk right now.

"Isn't it?" Grandad agreed. "I'm glad we were able to get this far before your mum and dad come to see us. This is a great spot – it's not too far from the road, though you'd never guess it, and there's a café with space to park cars over on the other side of that field. It's a popular mooring spot, so we're not allowed to stay here too long."

"You mean like you have to move on from parking spaces?" Anna asked, surprised. She hadn't realized it worked the same way for boats.

"Mm-hm. We can stay until Monday morning, but that's all."

Anna giggled. "It's not like the end of our road where you can only park for two hours, then!"

Grandad snorted. "Well, not quite."

"So – Mum and Dad will walk across here tomorrow, to come and see us?" Anna asked, with a tiny sigh.

"Yes. Are you OK, Anna?" Grandad looked at her worriedly. "I know you'll miss Fred, but he really will be happier back home, I think."

"Maybe," Anna agreed quietly. She couldn't help thinking that Fred would be happiest wherever she was. He was used to her being around, except when she was at school. And even then he would be at the front door to meet her as soon as she got back, flinging himself at her, barking and whining as if he'd thought he was never going to see her again.

Grandad gave her a sympathetic smile. "Look, why don't you take him for a really good run across that field now? Your gran's going to be a while cooking the dinner. You might even be able to let him off the lead – there doesn't seem to be anyone else around. Just don't go out of the field, though, will you? So that I know where you are?"

Anna nodded. "I promise. Come on, Fred!"

Fred looked over at the field hopefully, and his long tail swished slowly from side to side.

"Yes! Walk! Come on!" Anna patted her hand against her leg, and Fred leaped joyfully forward, prancing through the gate into the field. It was long, tussocky grass, and he and Anna raced across it, Anna laughing and stumbling as she tried to keep up with him.

"Slow down a minute! Fred, come on, stop. Then I can get your lead off. Yes, you see, silly, that's what you want, isn't it?" Fred danced about excitedly while Anna unclipped the lead, and then he bounded away, barking like a mad thing.

Anna watched him, giggling. She loved it when he ran so fast that his ears flapped. Today, he looked as though he might even take off.

Then she sighed and wrapped her arms around her middle. She knew that sending Fred home tomorrow was the sensible thing to do, but she still wasn't happy about it. And she didn't think Fred would be, either.

Chapter Five

Anna's mum and dad arrived the next day in time for lunch. They'd brought a lovely picnic with them, with loads of sandwiches and a chocolate cake, and they ate it under one of the oak trees in the big field. Then Dad and Anna played Frisbee with Fred, sending him racing across the field. Fred was excellent at catching the Frisbee – he did huge ballet-dancer leaps to grab it. But as the afternoon wore on, Anna kept thinking that Mum and Dad would have to go soon, and take Fred with them. She hardly ate any of the lasagne that Gran had made for dinner. Somehow she just didn't feel hungry.

"We should get back," Anna's dad said at last, peering at his watch. "We've got work tomorrow and it must be nearly your bedtime, Anna, even if it is the holidays. It's starting to get dark. But it's been a really good day."

Anna gulped and looked over at Fred, who was snoozing in the corner. He looked angelic – maybe Gran would say he could stay after all? But then she blew her hot fringe off her forehead, and remembered that it was so warm because the saloon doors were tightly closed. Closed to keep Fred in, so he didn't try to leap over the side of the boat. He'd nearly jumped into the canal again this morning, after he'd spotted a swan sailing grandly past.

"Do you want to gather Fred's stuff together?" Mum suggested gently. Then she saw Anna's worried face. "It'll be OK," she said. "I've got so much work done over the last few days, I can definitely take time off for some really good walks with Fred."

"I know," Anna murmured, picking up Fred's bowls and tipping his water into the kitchen sink. She polished them dry with some kitchen roll and started to fill the bag with all of Fred's things. One of the rubber bones squeaked as she picked it up, and Fred bounced up off his cushion, as though Anna had shouted his name.

He trotted over to her happily, waiting for her to throw him the toy. It was going to be difficult playing catch, with all these people squashed on to the boat, but it would still be fun.

But Anna just stared down at him sadly and put the squeaky bone into the bag that they'd brought with them to the boat. Fred watched her, confused, and then realized what this meant. Of course! They were going home! He wagged his tail so hard it thumped against Anna's legs, but for some reason she didn't look very happy.

Helpfully, he hurried back to his cushion and picked it up in his teeth, ready to go.

Dad laughed. "Look, Fred's keen to get in the car." He came over to Anna, and hugged her. "Don't worry, he'll be fine. I can take him for a walk after work, too, you know."

"I just think he'll miss me," Anna sniffed. Or maybe he wouldn't at all, and that would be almost worse.

Dad gave her a kiss and gathered up the bag, and Mum clipped on Fred's lead.

Anna and Gran and Grandad came out to the bow of the boat to wave goodbye, and even Sunny got up out of his basket to come and see what was going on.

Mum and Dad jumped over on to the bank, and Fred did a giant leap after them. He didn't look too worried, Anna thought sadly.

But then as Mum went to open the gate, Fred looked back and realized that Anna wasn't coming with them. He let out a little whine of surprise and stopped to wait for her.

"Come on, Fred!" Mum pulled gently on his lead, but Fred was pretty heavy when he didn't want to move.

"Oh..." Anna whispered. "He wants to stay."

She'd been wrong to think she'd be upset if he just walked away. It was much worse watching Fred turn his head from side to side, glancing anxiously between her and Mum and Dad, obviously not understanding what was going on. She wouldn't have minded if he'd trotted happily across the field, after all. She wished he had.

Mum pulled the lead a bit harder, and Fred lurched to his feet, padding unwillingly after her.

Anna started to cry, and Gran

hugged her. Even Sunny came over to her and pressed comfortingly against her leg. She turned her face into Gran's chest so she didn't have to watch.

Fred could hear Anna crying as Mum pulled him across the field and he hated it. He knew that was a bad noise – that it meant something was wrong. He didn't want Anna to sound like that, and he stopped suddenly, yanking at his lead so hard that he slipped his collar. He pulled even harder, dragging it over his ears, and then he was free.

Anna's mum had been holding the lead tightly, but when Fred got free she lost her balance and half fell over. "Fred, no! Come back! Bad dog!"

Fred flattened his ears and looked at

her worriedly. He'd done something wrong, he knew he had. But it couldn't really be wrong, because he needed to go and help Anna. He laid his ears back apologetically, and then he turned and raced back across the field to get to her.

"Fred, get back here!" Anna's dad yelled, dropping the bags and starting to chase after him. "No! Here!"

Fred flinched as he heard the shouting. He hated it when people shouted at him, and it seemed to have been happening all the time recently. Anna's grandad kept being cross with him, and now Dad was as well. He darted through the gate and saw Anna, still standing on the boat, watching sadly.

“Fred!” She leaned towards him, but Grandad was there, too, looking annoyed – and Sunny.

Sunny barked at him and Fred stopped, looking uncertainly at Anna. Then he heard Dad pounding up behind him and he skittered sideways along the path, not sure what to do. As Dad reached out to grab at him, he shot away up the towpath, and darted under the fence and into the shadows of the wood.

"What happened?" Anna gasped. "Fred was off his lead, Dad!"

Her dad nodded grimly. "He slipped his collar."

Mum hurried up to the gate. "You were right, Anna. He was upset about going without you."

Dad sighed. "I'll go and get him. Naughty thing!"

"Shall I come, too?" Anna suggested, putting her foot up on the side of the boat, ready to jump over to the bank.

Dad shook his head. "Better not. He's in a bit of a tizzy, isn't he? I don't want him getting any more excited."

Anna watched anxiously as Dad headed into the woods. Poor Fred. He really wouldn't understand what was happening. He was probably hiding under a bush somewhere, feeling even more miserable than she was.

Anna wriggled free of Gran's arms, and jumped out on to the bank. "I know Dad said to wait here, but I can't!" she told Mum. "I won't go into to the wood. I just want to see if Dad's found him yet."

She was pretty sure that he hadn't. She could hear him calling for Fred, and he was sounding more and more worried every time. Anna shivered as she came into the shadows of the trees hanging over the fence. It was getting late, after nine now, and the sun had set. It was almost dark.

A sudden, horrible thought made her stop, just as she was about to lean over the fence and peer in to look for Dad and Fred.

What if they didn't find him?

It was even darker in the wood, and Fred's red coat would blend into the shadows. If he was upset and hiding, Dad just wouldn't see him.

Anna gasped and climbed up on to the fence, trying to see through the dark trees.

"Anna!" Mum called. "Don't climb over there."

Anna twisted round to look at her. "Can't I go and help look? Please? Fred will come if I call him, Mum. He's scared, but he isn't scared of me."

"No, wait there." Mum dropped the bags and came over to her. "Dad will find him. He'll be back in a minute with Fred, I'm sure he will."

But just then, Dad came hurrying back up the thin thread of a path, a worried expression on his face. "I can't find him," he said anxiously. "The silly dog's gone racing off somewhere. I'm sorry, but I think we should all go and look and call for him. Have you got a torch?" he shouted across to Gran and Grandad.

Grandad nodded and went back into the boat. He returned with two big torches and handed one to Dad.

"My phone works as a torch as well," Mum said. "We'd better split up, then we can look everywhere. Anna, come with me, OK?"

Anna nodded. She was too upset to say anything. Her beautiful Fred was lost, hiding somewhere in this horrible wood, all alone.

Fred huddled in a hole under the roots of a tree, watching the trees get darker and darker in front of him. He wasn't exactly sure where he was, but he thought he could find his way back to the boat. He'd gone quite far, racing as fast as he could away from Sunny and all the angry people shouting at him. But he could always follow his own scent back the way he'd run.

He just wasn't sure that he wanted to go back. Not yet, anyway. Dad had been trying to take him away from Anna, and he didn't understand why.

Fred snuffled at the dusty leaf litter in the bottom of his hiding place. What else could he do? He didn't want to stay here. It was getting dark and even though he could see quite well in the dim light, he didn't like it much. He wanted to be sitting on his comfortable cushion, with Anna stroking his ears.

Fred's ears twitched. There were footsteps coming down the path. He wriggled uncertainly and poked his nose out of the hole. Someone was calling for him! Fred was about to jump out and see who it was when he recognized the voice. It was Grandad, sounding worried and calling, "Here, Fred! Fred! Come on, boy!"

Fred listened and then he scrunched back up into his hiding place, making himself small. Grandad had been cross with him back on the boat, and Fred could hear the strain in his voice now, too.

He wouldn't go back just yet. Not while people were still cross. He'd stay hidden a little while longer.

Chapter Six

"But we can't stop looking!" Anna stared up at them all in horror.

"It's too dark," Dad explained. "We can hardly see, even with the torches, sweetheart."

"Someone could trip over. If you put your foot in a rabbit hole you could break an ankle," Mum added, putting her hands on Anna's shoulders.

"I know you want to find Fred, and I'm really sorry. But we just aren't going to find him like this," said Gran.

Anna shook her head, looking back out at the dark trees. "We can't leave him out there all night. He'll be scared!" She took the torch out of Dad's hand, and started to flash it around the path again, calling for Fred. Her voice sounded hoarse and her throat hurt, she'd been shouting for so long. "There's a noise!" she gasped, starting forward excitedly. "A rustling, can't you hear it? It has to be Fred!"

But when the creature came out from between the trees, it stopped in surprise, instead of running to greet them. Anna's torch flashed on to a pair of frightened, glowing eyes. She rushed to hug it, but the fox whisked away, its red bushy tail nothing like Fred's beautiful feathers.

“It wasn’t him,” Anna whispered miserably.

“It was only a fox,” Gran nodded, as Anna sagged with disappointment, her shoulders drooping. “Anna, it’s so late, you’re exhausted. We’ve been searching for two hours now. You need to go to bed. We all do. Your mum and dad have still got to drive back.”

“But Fred…”

“I think he’s upset and he’s hiding,” Dad explained, hugging her. “We can start looking again tomorrow. We’ll get up really early and come straight here. I’ll just have to go into work late. Fred’s not used to the dark, is he? When it’s light he’ll feel better and come out. He’ll want to come back to us then.”

“I want him back now!” Anna sobbed.

She hated the thought of Fred being too scared to come and find her.

"We all do," Dad said, but Anna couldn't help thinking he was only saying that. If he really wanted Fred back, they'd keep looking all night.

"Just one more look," she begged, pulling away. Then her feet seemed to wobble underneath her and everything went blurry. Someone grabbed her and she heard Mum's voice. It seemed to be coming from a long way away.

"Anna, you're asleep on your feet! Come on."

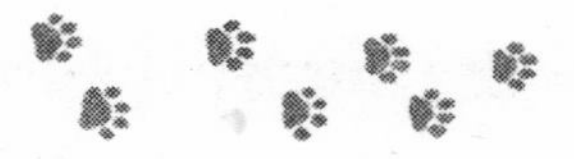

Anna lay in her little bed, worrying. Even though she'd been almost asleep out in the wood, now she felt horribly awake. She kept putting her hand out to stroke Fred to make her feel better, and then she'd realize all over again that he wasn't there.

The boat rocked a little, and she sat up, looking hopefully at the door. "Did you find him?" she gasped, as Gran and Grandad came in. She had been so upset when they took her back to the boat that Grandad had promised to go and have one last look if she would be sensible and get into bed.

"No, Anna, I'm sorry," said Grandad. "But I was thinking – Irish Setters are good trackers, they were bred for hunting. I'm pretty sure Fred will find his own way back. We'll probably see him sitting in the front of the boat, watching the ducks in the morning!"

"Or he'll wake us up at four o'clock scratching at the door," Gran put in, perching on the end of Anna's bed.

"You really think so?" Anna sniffed.

Gran hesitated, just for a second, but Anna had felt it.

"What I think is that you need to get to sleep," Gran said quickly. "If we do have to go looking for Fred tomorrow morning, you'll want to be up early. We're going to bed now, too."

Anna listened to them fussing around getting ready for bed, and gradually everything grew quiet. But she still couldn't sleep. If only Sunny and Fred had got on better, this would never have happened. But now poor Fred had been driven away.

Everyone had tried to tell her that it would be fine – that Fred would be back soon, or that they'd at least find him tomorrow morning. Anna wanted so much to believe that they were right, but she couldn't help thinking about what might happen if they weren't.

Where was Fred? What if he'd run all the way through the wood to the road? Mum and Anna had been through the wood and seen the cars roaring past…

Anna shivered. Surely Fred wouldn't have gone out into the road, would he? He was used to walking in town, and they'd been careful to train him to stop and sit at the edge of the pavement. But what if he didn't see what it was in the dark? It was a country road, with a grassy verge and no kerb. He might not realize it was a road at all.

Anna rolled over and buried her face in the pillow to try to stop herself crying. But she couldn't hold back the tears seeping out of the corners of her eyes.

Fred could get run over. What would she do if she never saw him again?

Fred stuck his muzzle out of the gap

under the tree roots and sniffed cautiously. He'd never been out this late before. He wriggled out of his hiding place and shook himself. His legs felt strange, cramped up and wobbly. He walked slowly around in a little circle, sniffing for the scent trail back to the boat. He was jittery and upset, and it seemed harder to find a scent than it usually was. But at last he found it and began to trot back through the wood.

He wriggled under the fence and came back out on to the canal bank. He could see the boat, looming up out of the canal like a darker patch of shadow. Fred slunk across the grass towards it, not sure what to do. The boat was quiet and all the lights were out. Everyone was asleep, perhaps. They might shout at him again if he woke them up. He went up closer, standing on the edge of the bank, his ears twitching as he tried to listen for Anna.

Quietly, carefully, he jumped into the deck well at the bow of the boat. He could stay here till the morning, he thought. And Anna would see him when she woke up. But then he heard a shifting, creaking noise from inside, and paws padded over towards the door.

He had forgotten about Sunny.

There was a low, uncertain growl from the other side of the door and Fred backed away miserably, bumping up against the side of the boat.

He jumped back on to the bank, his paws scrabbling a little against the damp, slippery grass, and padded away. He needed Anna, but he couldn't get to her without going past Sunny first. He would have to wait until morning, he decided wearily. All of him ached after the hours curled up in that uncomfortable hole. And he was so tired.

Fred wandered along the bank, sniffing at the other two boats on the mooring. He couldn't smell any dogs on either of them. Cautiously, he put his paws up on the side of the hull of the last boat and looked in at the stern well. There was a canvas awning folded up, and he jumped lightly down into the boat, wriggling under it and curling up, fidgeting to settle his aching paws.

Then, at last, he fell asleep.

Chapter Seven

Anna had strange, horrible dreams all night. She and Sunny and Fred went round and round in circles, chasing each other, and however hard Anna ran, she seemed to be standing still. In the worst dream, which seemed to keep coming back, she and Fred both had wings, and Anna was flapping and flapping and trying to catch up with him, but he was always too fast.

She woke up with a jolt, gasping for breath. The dream seemed so real that she expected her arms to ache. She stretched them out gingerly, but they felt just like they usually did.

"You're awake, Anna!" Gran bustled over to her. "I was about to get you up."

Anna blinked and then looked around, her fingers clenching on her bedcover. "He's not back, is he?" she asked, her voice very small. She knew he wasn't. He'd have been all over her by now, barking and licking.

Gran sighed. "No. No, he isn't yet."

"What time is it?" Anna asked, jumping out of bed and starting to pull on her clothes. It didn't look like early morning – the sun was bright already, and Gran was dressed and making breakfast.

"It's eight o'clock. Oh, I know you wanted to wake up early, Anna, but you were so tired, and you were up so late last night."

Anna stared at her in horror. How could they have let her sleep for so long? "I have to go out and look for Fred!" she gasped, hopping her way into her jeans.

"Grandad's been out for a while, searching the wood again," her gran explained. "And your mum and dad will be here soon to help as well. They said they'd just go and walk along the road that runs by the back of the wood first."

Anna nodded miserably. So it wasn't just her worrying that Fred had gone further than the wood.

"We'll have to move the boat this morning as well," her gran said gently.

Anna yanked her sweater over her head and turned to look at Gran in horror. She'd forgotten that they couldn't stay on the mooring. "We've still got to go?" she whispered. "We have to leave Fred behind?"

"We won't go far, I promise. Just a little further up the canal. Grandad says he's sure there's somewhere we can stop and moor up, about a mile further on from here. Then we'll hurry back."

Anna nodded, but she felt like howling. Somehow it seemed like giving up on Fred, even though she knew they were coming back.

The boat shook a little as Grandad stepped back on board, and he came in through the saloon door.

Anna opened her mouth to ask, but Grandad shook his head. "No sign at the moment, Anna, sorry. But your mum called, saying they've parked over where they were last night. They're going to walk along to the village and go into the shops to ask if anyone's seen him." He eyed Anna anxiously and added, "They printed out a few posters, too."

"But Fred's only been gone one night..." Anna said, shaking her head. "He's not really lost, is he? We don't need posters up!" Putting up posters made it feel all the more real.

Grandad shook his head. "I know what you mean, but if someone sees Fred and doesn't realize he's lost – if they just think he's off the lead and they can't see his owner, they won't do anything, will they? People will know to be looking out for him if they see a poster."

"I suppose so," Anna murmured. She was glad Mum and Dad hadn't come to the boat before they set off with the posters. She was pretty sure that a LOST poster with Fred's photo on it would have turned her into a wobbly, crying mess. And she'd be no use to Fred like that. She shook herself briskly and sniffed.

"If I take a piece of toast with me, can I go and look for him now? Just one more quick look before we have to move the boat? Please? I'll be back soon."

Gran and Grandad exchanged glances, but then Gran said, "If you're careful. Stay on the path, Anna, though, won't you?"

Anna nodded eagerly, snatching up the toast and heading for the door. Sunny thumped his tail against his basket as she went past, and Anna stopped to pat him quickly. She'd felt furious with him last night, while she was lying there worrying about Fred. But it wasn't really his fault. He just liked things his own way, nice and quiet, without a big, bouncy puppy jumping all over him.

She leaped from the boat to the towpath, and headed back into the wood. It looked so different this morning, with sunlight pouring in through the gaps in the trees. It wasn't the eerie, almost frightening place it had been the night before. There were birds singing, and as Anna hurried down the path, a tiny rabbit suddenly turned tail and disappeared into the bracken.

Anna's mouth twitched into half a smile. Even though she felt awful, the rabbit's surprised expression had been so funny. Then she stopped and looked around thoughtfully. Fred would have chased that rabbit, if he'd seen it. He would have jumped after it, barking so loudly that the rabbit and all of its friends and relations would be hiding in their burrows in seconds. That rabbit hopping calmly around on the path made Anna think that Fred wasn't anywhere near.

She gulped and swallowed. Maybe he was long gone, then. Maybe he had gone out on to the road, and Mum and Dad had the right idea to go there first.

Anna turned and headed back to the boat. Maybe if Mum and Dad weren't too far away, she could go and find them and help them look while Gran and Grandad moved the *Hummingbird*. She couldn't bear the thought of going further away and wasting all that time.

"Hello!" Grandad waved to her from the towpath as she came out of the trees. "I'm just going to walk up and ask the people on the other boats to watch out for Fred. Do you want to come?"

Anna nodded. She didn't want to, actually. She hated the thought of telling people that Fred was lost. Like the posters, it made it seem as though he really was. But she'd do anything to get him back, she told herself.

The people on the next boat were sitting on their bow deck, drinking tea, so it was easy to talk to them.

Anna liked that about being out on the canal – everyone seemed very friendly. Even when someone had made a mistake and messed up going into a lock, people would always come and help instead of getting annoyed.

"What, your lovely Irish Setter?" the lady asked, as Grandad explained.

"Yes," said Grandad. "We're especially worried as we've got to move on from the mooring this morning. We're going to stop a little bit further on and walk back, but just in case we miss him, it would be great if you could keep an eye out. Here's our mobile number."

"Of course we'll look out for him," said the lady, taking the piece of paper. "Oh dear, how awful for you."

The man frowned thoughtfully. "I don't think the people on the next boat are up yet," he said, glancing over. The boat at the end still had its curtains drawn and there was no noise from it at all. "Want us to tell them for you?"

"Please." Grandad nodded. "Thanks, you've been really helpful."

Anna tried to smile at the friendly

couple, but she just couldn't make her face do it. "Are we going now?" she asked Grandad, as she climbed back on to the *Hummingbird*.

Grandad nodded and headed for the stern to start the engine. "Yes, I think it's best. We can come back and spend the whole day here looking if we need to. But I'm sure we won't," he added quickly.

Anna could tell he didn't believe that at all, but she was just grateful to him for saying it.

"I wouldn't be surprised if we had a call from your mum and dad really soon," Gran said comfortingly. "I'm sure they'll have news."

"The engine's warmed up enough now," Grandad called from the stern, and Anna took one last, hopeful look along the bank, but no feathery, dark-red dog came running out to her.

"Let's go," she said. Then she coughed to clear her throat and said it again, loud enough to be heard over the engine this time. "The sooner we go, the sooner we can come back and start looking for Fred again."

Grandad nodded, and Anna hopped over on to the towpath to cast off the mooring ropes. Then she climbed back on to the bow deck. Gran had gone into the cabin, but Anna decided to stay out on deck. She felt like being on her own for a bit.

"We'll be back really soon, Fred," she whispered. "I'm not leaving you behind. We're coming back to find you."

Chapter Eight

Sunny felt the boat start to move away from the bank. He climbed out of his basket and came to stand next to Anna, putting his paws up on the bench seat that ran round the side of the bow and peering over the side.

Anna stroked his black head and sighed. "I wish you could help us find Fred, Sunny. Couldn't you sniff him out for me?" Then she frowned. "I wonder if you could? I'll have to ask Grandad. If you did, I promise we'd take him straight home – no more Fred trying to make you play chase. Honest."

Then she sniffed. She'd give anything to be chasing around the park with Fred now. She wouldn't even mind being stuck at home, bored, while Mum was working, just as long as Fred was there with her.

"I shouldn't have said yes to coming on the boat, should I?" she said to Sunny, tears rolling slowly down her cheeks. "It wasn't fair on you or Fred." She gave Sunny a last pat, and then climbed up on to the little bench. She lifted her hand to shield her eyes from the sun, scanning the bank eagerly as they drew away into the middle of the canal and began to sail slowly around the bend. The other boats hid the bank, and Anna suddenly couldn't bear that they were leaving. Fred was still there, somewhere! "Fred!" she yelled, again and again. But he didn't come. Anna put her hands over her eyes and cried.

Fred felt the thrumming sound of the engine more than he heard it. He was so tired after his frightened dash away through the woods, and his hours cramped up underneath the tree, that he'd slept far later than he usually would.

His first thought when the engine growled was that he was very, very hungry and why hadn't Anna come to find him for some breakfast? He would go and look for her right now. He twitched and stretched under the canvas awning, pushing his front paws out along the deck. But the feel of the heavy canvas over his head and shoulders was wrong, and his legs still ached a little. As he began to wake up properly, he had the feeling that something wasn't right.

Then he remembered.

He wasn't with Anna. He was on the other boat, hiding. The wrong boat! And that growling loudness was the sound that boats made when they moved! He had to get off, now, before this boat took him away from Anna!

Frantically, he scrambled out from beneath the awning and dashed to the side of the boat. Then a great shudder of relief ran through him, and his tail swished gladly back and forth. The boat was still moored up against the bank. It hadn't moved, even though he'd heard the engine noise.

Fred half-jumped, half-scrabbled his way out on to the bank. He needed to get back to Anna. Even if it meant Sunny growling at him and Grandad and everyone else being angry, he didn't care. Anna was what mattered. Even if she was cross with him, he wouldn't mind, as long as she was there. He'd missed her, and he was hungry, and he wanted *her* to feed him. No one else.

Fred pranced down the towpath, his tail wafting happily. Should he jump straight back on to the boat, or should he bark and let Anna see him and call him on board? If he barked, he might set Sunny off growling at him. Perhaps it would be best to just jump into that little bit of the boat outside the door, and sit quietly and wait?

He hurried eagerly along past another boat and looked curiously at the people sitting on it. The lady got to her feet and waved her arms at him. But Fred ran on.

Then he stopped, staring at the space where Anna's boat was meant to be.

They had gone. Without him.

Anna had left him behind. Fred walked to the edge of the bank, somehow hoping that he was wrong and the boat was there after all. But it definitely wasn't. That had been the engine noise he'd heard – it had been them leaving.

He could still hear it. Not too loud, but there. Perhaps they had only just gone? Fred leaned out over the edge of the bank, trying to see, his paws scrabbling on the grass. There they were! He could even just make out Anna, standing at the front of the boat.

He was about to bark, to tell her to come back for him, when he saw that Sunny was with her. She was stroking his head. Running her fingers over Sunny's ears, the way she did with his.

Fred watched, his tail sinking down between his legs. She wanted Sunny instead of him. He had caused so much trouble, and knocked things over, and made people shout at him. Anna's mum and dad had taken him away because she didn't want him any more.

But then, just as the boat began to turn, Anna suddenly stepped up on to something. Fred could see her better now. Sunny disappeared, and Anna stood there, peering at the bank as though she was looking for something.

For him?

She was crying. She was brushing tears away from her eyes, and she was calling... He could only just hear her over the engine noise, but he was sure that she was. Her voice had gone all growly and strange – the way it was when she was upset.

Fred barked and whipped round, racing down the bank after them. He hardly heard the lady on the next boat calling him frantically as she climbed over on to the bank. He didn't realize that she was trying to catch him as he shot past her. He only knew that he had to get to Anna.

The *Hummingbird* was pulling around the shallow bend in the canal now. Fred barked and barked as he ran, and he saw Anna look round and spot him.

"Fred!" she screamed excitedly. "Grandad, stop! Fred's there!"

Grandad turned to look at the bank and swung the tiller over to move in towards it. But the heavy boat took time to change course, and to Fred it didn't seem to be changing direction at all. He could see that Anna was shouting and waving, and she didn't look cross with him at all. But why wasn't she coming back for him?

Maybe she couldn't…?

Fred watched the boat for a couple more seconds, seeing it still drawing further down the canal. Taking Anna away from him.

Then he jumped into the water.

The water was cold and dark and unwelcoming and he didn't want to be in it at all. But if it was the only way he could get back to Anna, then that was what he would do.

He paddled away with his front paws. This was the first time he had ever been in deep water, and he could feel the weight of it in his coat, dragging him down. And no matter how hard he tried, he didn't seem to be getting very far. The cold seemed to sink straight into his cramped legs, but he kept paddling as hard as he could.

"He's in the water!" Anna screamed. "Grandad, where's the life-ring?" But

Grandad couldn't hear her shouting over the noise of the engine. Anna would have to fetch the life-ring herself. There was no time to lose. She spotted the life-ring attached to the roof and leaned over to reach it.

Grandad had told her never to walk round the narrow shelf that ran round the outside of the boat, but it was the only way she could get close enough to Fred to throw him the heavy life-ring. She hooked it over her arm and stepped out on to the shelf, gripping the rail that ran along the roof of the boat.

As she edged her way round, she could see Fred struggling as he hit the *Hummingbird*'s wake. He gasped and snorted as he swallowed a great mouthful of water.

"I think he's sinking," Anna wailed, clinging on to the rail with one hand. She threw the life-ring as close to Fred as she could, but it fell short. She started to haul it back, glancing worriedly at Fred still struggling in the rough water thrown up behind the boat.

Maybe I should just go in after him, Anna thought, starting to pull off her shoes. She could swim pretty well, even though she knew the canal was nothing like a nice heated swimming pool. Grandad could throw her the life-ring and pull them both in. There was no way she was going to let Fred drown.

But then a black shape shot past her and there was another huge splash, followed by a steady sound of paddling, as Sunny cut through the water.

"Go on, Sunny!" Anna yelled.

Gran hurried out on to the bow deck. "What's going on? I just saw Sunny jump into the canal! Anna, come back down off there!"

"It's Fred!" Anna pointed into the water. "Sunny's rescuing him!"

"Oh my goodness," Gran murmured. "Geoff, look!" she called, banging on the cabin roof. "The dogs are in the canal."

Grandad looked out across the water and his eyes widened. He waved back and steered the boat into the bank.

They all watched as Sunny paddled calmly round behind the boat and up to Fred, who was gasping and struggling in the cold water. The puppy rolled his eyes sideways, wondering what Sunny was doing. He whined as he felt Sunny grab the folds of skin at the scruff of his neck. But he didn't pull away. He could feel that Sunny was helping him. Once he'd got a good hold on Fred, Sunny turned, swimming him back towards the bank.

Anna jumped off the boat as soon as it drew into the side, stumbling as she hit the grass.

"Go and help them," Gran called, grabbing the ropes and stepping after her. "Don't worry. I'll hold on to these."

Grandad shut off the engine and jumped after Anna, and they ran down the bank, just as Sunny and Fred were reaching the side.

"Good dog, Sunny! Come on!" Grandad yelled. "Good boy!"

"Come on, Fred!" Anna called, watching him anxiously. He was so still in Sunny's grip, she couldn't even tell if he was breathing. But as Sunny bumped him gently against the bank, Fred seemed to wake up, scrabbling frantically for dry land. Grandad put his arms under Fred's front legs and hauled him on to the bank, where Fred wriggled gratefully on to Anna's knees. She hugged him tightly.

Sunny leaped out with a helping heave from Grandad and shook himself all over. Then he leaned down and sniffed at Fred, nudging him up.

Fred struggled up obediently, shaking the water out of his coat. Sunny pulled at the leg of Anna's jeans with his teeth, so that she got to her feet, too. Then he set off back to the boat, herding them like a sheepdog, circling round Fred and Anna as they walked back down the towpath.

"What are you doing, Sunny?" Anna giggled.

"He wants everybody safely back on the boat," Grandad said, chuckling.

"He rescued Fred," Anna murmured. She could feel her cold, damp dog shivering against her legs. She was almost sure that Fred wouldn't have made it out of the canal on his own. And she was only realizing now how amazing the rescue had been.

"Sunny doesn't even like Fred!"

Grandad nodded thoughtfully. "He may not like Fred fussing at him, but Fred's part of his family, I suppose."

"I've got towels," Gran called. "I've tied the boat to those trees, just for the minute. Come inside. We'll get the dogs dried off and I'll make some tea."

Sunny stood watchfully by as Anna helped Fred back on to the boat. Then she and Grandad dried the dogs with the old towels Gran had found.

Gran passed Anna a mug of sweet hot chocolate, and looked down worriedly at the two dogs. "I wish we could give them a hot drink, too."

"Fred looks a lot better now he's drier," Anna said, sipping at her hot chocolate. Fred was leaning against her lovingly and she could feel that he wasn't shivering so much. "Oh! We have to call Mum and Dad! We have to tell them we've got Fred back. And that Sunny's a hero dog."

Sunny shook his way out of the towel that Grandad had wrapped round him and stood up, shaking his ears as though they still felt watery. Then he nudged Fred with his muzzle again.

Fred wriggled back to his feet. He licked Anna's cheek lovingly, but he followed Sunny into the saloon, towards Sunny's big wicker basket. Fred stood looking at it uncertainly, his tail waving a little. He knew he wasn't meant to go in Sunny's basket. But the bigger dog pushed him gently into it and climbed in after him, curling up round the Setter puppy as though he was trying to keep him warm.

Sunny glanced at them all, and then let out a deep, huffing sigh and closed his eyes, as though he was finally happy with where everyone was.

"Look at them!" Anna whispered, crouching down to see. "You're right, Grandad. Sunny's decided that Fred's his family now."

Fred peered over the edge of the basket, making sure Anna was still there. He stretched, and wriggled a little, and licked her hand. He was back, and Anna was with him, and everything was all right. Then he snuggled up against the big dog and went to sleep.

Glossary

Awning – a sheet of material that you put over a boat to stop it getting wet inside

Bank – the side of a river or canal

Bow – the front of a boat

Canal – a manmade waterway for boats to travel down

Cast off – to untie a boat so that it can sail away

Hull – the main part of the boat that sits in the water

Lock – a section of a canal with gates at each end, used for raising or lowering boats

Moor – to tie up a boat to the side of a river or canal

Stern – the back of a boat

Tiller – a lever used to steer a boat

Towpath – a path beside a river or canal, originally used as a pathway for horses pulling boats

Wake – waves made by a moving boat